Crazy about puppies?

Murphy loves swimming in rivers, but how will he feel when faced with the sea?

Want to know about real life assistance dogs?

'A must for any children hooked on animals or school stories'
- TELEGRAPH

Welcome to Sausage Dreams **PUPPY ACADEMY**, where a team of plucky young pups are learning how to be all sorts of working dogs. Let's meet some of the students...

MURPHY
the BiG ONE!

BREED Leonberger
SPECIAL SKILL
Swimming

Scout
THE SMART ONE!

BREED German shepherd

SPECIAL SKILL
Sniffing out crime

STAR
THE SPEEDY ONE!

BREED Border collie

SPECIAL SKILL
Sensing danger

PiP
THE FRIENDLY ONE!

BREED Labrador

SPECIAL SKILL
Ball games

...and some of the teachers:

MAJOR BONES

One of the teachers at the
Sausage Dreams **Puppy Academy**.
Known for being strict.

PROFESSOR OFFENBACH

Head of the Sausage Dreams **Puppy Academy.** She is a small dog with A VERY LOUD VOICE!

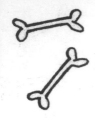

OXFORD
UNIVERSITY PRESS

Great Clarendon Street, Oxford OX2 6DP

Oxford University Press is a department of the University of Oxford.
It furthers the University's objective of excellence in research, scholarship,
and education by publishing worldwide in

Oxford New York

Auckland Cape Town Dar es Salaam Hong Kong Karachi
Kuala Lumpur Madrid Melbourne Mexico City Nairobi
New Delhi Shanghai Taipei Toronto

With offices in

Argentina Austria Brazil Chile Czech Republic France Greece
Guatemala Hungary Italy Japan Poland Portugal Singapore
South Korea Switzerland Thailand Turkey Ukraine Vietnam

Oxford is a registered trade mark of Oxford University Press
in the UK and in certain other countries

British Library Cataloguing in Publication Data

Data available

ISBN: 978-0-19-273926-1

GILL LEWIS

PUPPY ACADEMY

ILLUSTRATED BY SARAH HORNE

MURPHY

AND THE GREAT SURF RESCUE

OXFORD
UNIVERSITY PRESS

1

'Help! Help!'

The small Labrador puppy splashed in the middle of the river.

The pups on the riverbank barked frantically.

'Pip's in trouble!' woofed Scruff.

Pip splashed one more time before his head slipped under the water.

There was nothing they could do.

'Oh no!' yipped Star. 'He's gone.'

A few bubbles rose to the surface

of the water, then all was still.

'Who can save him?' barked
Scruff.

'WOOF!'

A big brown blur whizzed through
the air.

The pups cheered. 'Save him,
Murphy,' they shouted. 'Save him.'

Murphy hit the water.

SPLASH!!

He knew what he had to do.
His huge webbed paws pulled him
forward. His thick fur kept him
warm. He swam and swam to the
middle of the river.

He had to save Pip.

He had to.

But time was running out.

Murphy put his head beneath
the water, grabbed Pip's collar, and
pulled him to the surface.

'Come on, Murphy,' barked the
pups on the shore. 'You can do it.'

Murphy paddled back to them,
keeping Pip's head
above the water.
He was
almost there.

Almost!

His paws touched the soft mud.
His claws gripped the ground and he
pulled Pip out onto the riverbank.

The other pups bounced all around
him. 'Hooray for Murphy,' they
barked. 'You did it. You saved Pip.'

But Murphy was worried. Had he
saved Pip in time?

He looked across at Major Bones
who was holding up his stopwatch.

Major Bones was a teacher at the Sausage Dreams Academy for Working Dogs.

'Thank you, Pip, for pretending to be our pup in trouble today. I can now reveal Murphy's result.'

All the pups fell silent.

Murphy waited. The river water dripped from his fur and pooled in great puddles around his paws.

'Well, Murphy,' barked Major Bones, 'congratulations. You've passed your Level One River Rescue. And,' he added, 'you rescued Pip in two minutes and five seconds. That's a new record for the academy.'

The pups cheered.

'You're the champion,' woofed Star, 'the best!'

Murphy puffed out his chest in pride. He was a Leonberger pup. One day he would grow into a huge lion-like dog. His ancestors were Newfoundlands, which had once been bred to help fishermen in icy waters. Murphy had water rescue in his blood.

Murphy did what he did best after swimming.

He shook himself, starting at his nose, and then his head, and shaking out his chest and body, and then his tail, spraying water over everyone.

'Hey! Watch out!' yelped Star. 'You've got most of the river in your fur. We'll *all* look like we've half-drowned today.'

Pip jumped up and bounced back into the river. 'Save me again, Murphy,' he barked. 'That was fun. Save me again.' He swam around in circles, pretending to drown.

'No, save me,' barked Star, 'it's my turn.'

'I want to be saved by Murphy,' woofed Scruff.

Major Bones stood up. 'That's it for today, pups. It's time to get back. If we hurry, we might be able to slip Murphy into the Friday award ceremony.'

Murphy and the other pups trotted back to the Sausage Dreams Puppy Academy for Working Dogs. They were all in the same class. At the Puppy Academy, pups trained for all sorts of important jobs, such as guide dogs, sheep dogs, and search and rescue dogs. Some pups hadn't even decided what they wanted to be yet.

But Murphy knew.

He knew from the very first moment he had seen Boris of Bognor Regis on Dog TV, flying across the sand with the sun on his coat and the wind in his ears.

Boris was a Newfoundland surf rescue dog. He was the only dog to have ever been awarded the gold medal of gallantry for saving someone in peril at sea.

Boris was *everyone's* hero.
Murphy wanted to be just like him.
He wanted to be a hero too.

9

2

'**SILENCE PLEASE!**' yapped
Professor Offenbach. '**AND SIT!**'

Murphy sat next to his friends
in the hall. Some of the smaller
pups covered their ears. Professor
Offenbach was the head of the
Puppy Academy. No one knew how
such a loud sound could come from
such a small dog. She could be heard
from two miles away when she was
really cross.

Star nudged Murphy and pointed to a new pup in the hall. 'Who's that?'

Murphy stared at the pup. He looked different from the other pups at the academy. He had no fur except for tufts on his head and tail, and at the ends of his four paws. 'I don't know,' he whispered.

'It looks like we're going to find out,' said Scruff. 'Look, Professor Offenbach is

calling him over.'

'BEFORE I GIVE OUT THE AWARDS FOR TODAY'S FRIDAY CEREMONY, I WOULD LIKE TO GIVE A WARM WELCOME TO A NEW MEMBER OF THE ACADEMY. WE ARE VERY LUCKY TO HAVE RODRIGO LOPEZ VISITING US FOR A SHORT WHILE.'

Rodrigo gave a small wave to the puppies.

'RODRIGO HAS COME ALL THE WAY FROM MEXICO. I'M SURE YOU WILL ALL MAKE RODRIGO FEEL VERY WELCOME

HERE, AND HOPE YOU TAKE THE
OPPORTUNITY TO FIND OUT
ABOUT HIS COUNTRY.'

'Why's he visiting us?' whispered
Star.

'SOME OF YOU MAY BE
WONDERING WHY RODRIGO
IS HERE,' woofed the
professor. 'RODRIGO WILL BE
REPRESENTING HIS COUNTRY AT
THE WORLD JUNIOR SURF-DOG
CHAMPIONSHIPS TOMORROW
AT BLUE FLAG BEACH. HE WILL
ALSO BE CONTINUING HIS
WATER RESCUE TRAINING WITH
US HERE AT THE ACADEMY.

RODRIGO
HOLDS
THE
INTERNATIONAL
RECORD FOR THE
LEVEL ONE RIVER RESCUE,
IN AN ASTONISHING TIME OF
ONE MINUTE AND FORTY-FIVE
SECONDS.'

Pip turned to Murphy. 'Wow,' he said. 'That's even faster than you.'

Murphy scowled. 'I could have rescued you faster than that, if you hadn't swum so far out into the river.'

Scruff tried to get a better view

of the new pup. 'And he surfs too! That's pretty cool!'

'Pfff!' said Murphy. 'Surfing's no big deal. It's just standing on a plank of wood in the water.'

But Murphy's friends weren't listening to him. They were more interested in Rodrigo Lopez, the new pup in the school.

'AND NOW FOR THE FRIDAY AWARDS. LET'S CELEBRATE THIS WEEK'S ACHIEVEMENTS,' boomed Professor Offenbach.

Murphy watched Bertie the basset hound receive the Golden Nose award for following a scent trail for

two miles through the woods. He
watched Carly the collie collect the
Bo-Peep badge for herding Hilda
and Mabel, the academy sheep. He
watched Lily the labradoodle collect
the Doorbell prize for alerting a deaf
human to someone at the door.

All the time, Murphy couldn't
help glancing at the new dog. Could
Rodrigo really be that good at water
rescue? Could he be better than
Murphy? Maybe the other pups would
like Rodrigo more. He was probably

one big show-off. Murphy began to wish Rodrigo had never come to the academy.

Professor Offenbach rolled up her piece of paper.

Murphy sighed. Maybe he wouldn't receive his award this week.

'AND LAST BUT NOT LEAST . . .' yapped Professor Offenbach. 'MURPHY, FOR HIS LEVEL ONE RIVER RESCUE BADGE.'

Scruff prodded Murphy with her paw. 'Go on,' she said. 'Go and get your badge.'

Murphy joined Bertie, Carly, and Lily on the giant sausage podium.

'**WELL DONE,**' barked Professor Offenbach. She clipped the badge on Murphy's collar. '**MAJOR BONES SAYS YOU ARE READY FOR THE NEXT TEST. NEXT WEEK YOU**

WILL JOIN RODRIGO AT BLUE
FLAG BEACH BEFORE THE
SURFING CHAMPIONSHIPS TO
TRY FOR YOUR SURF RESCUE
BADGE.'

Murphy wagged his tail, although
he secretly wished Rodrigo didn't
have to come too.

'AND I'VE JUST HEARD,'
continued Professor Offenbach,
'THAT YOUR INSTRUCTOR ON
THE BEACH WILL BE NONE
OTHER THAN THE WORLD
FAMOUS . . . '

Murphy could feel excitement
fizz right through him. His whiskers

trembled. He didn't dare to hope too much.

Professor Offenbach raised her voice even higher '. . . THE ONE AND ONLY . . . THE SURF RESCUE HERO . . . BORIS OF BOGNOR REGIS.'

3

The pups packed towels and picnics into the minibus.

'We're so lucky we can all come too,' said Scruff.

Professor Offenbach had given all the pups a day at the beach to watch the World Junior Surf-Dog Championships. Murphy and Rodrigo would try for their Surf Rescue badge in the morning before the surfing competition began.

'Look,' said Star, 'here comes Rodrigo.'

Murphy watched as the new pup struggled with his surfboard and bags to the minibus.

'Come on,' said Pip. 'Let's give him a paw.'

Murphy stayed behind and watched Scruff, Star, and Pip bound over to Rodrigo. They weren't the only ones wanting to help him. Other pups crowded around Rodrigo too. Between them, Scruff and Pip

carried the surfboard, and the other
pups held onto bags and towels.

Murphy picked up his own bag
and climbed onto the minibus.
What was so special about Rodrigo?
He flumped down on a seat and
hoped his friends would join him.
Many pups took seats around
Rodrigo, but Star, Scruff, and Pip sat
down next to Murphy.

'Have you seen Rodrigo's
surfboard?' said Star.

'It was designed by Salty Old Sea

Dogs, the best surfboard makers in the world,' said Scruff.

'Rodrigo says it's a triple finned shortboard, for faster turns on the waves,' said Pip.

Murphy pretended to yawn. 'Wow, that's sounds *really* interesting.' He turned round to look at Rodrigo. Rodrigo's sun-bleached fur flopped over his eyes.

'He looks pretty cool, doesn't he?' sighed Scruff.

Murphy snorted. 'More like a rat with a bad-hair day.'

'Murphy!' said Star. 'That's a mean thing to say.'

'Well, look at him,' said Murphy. 'He's got hardly any fur on him.'

'He's not supposed to,' said Pip. 'He's a Mexican hairless dog.'

'Brainless too, probably,' muttered Murphy.

'Don't be like that,' said Star. 'He seems nice, and really friendly.'

'He's a great surf-dog too,' said Pip.

Murphy scowled and turned away. 'If he's so wonderful, why don't you go and sit with him instead.'

Star grabbed her bag and got up. She looked at Murphy with hurt in her eyes. 'Well, maybe we will.' She turned to the others. 'Come on, let's go and see Rodrigo. I'm not sure we're welcome here.'

Star, Scruff, and Pip moved seats, leaving Murphy on his own, all alone.

Murphy could see Major Bones glancing back at him, but Murphy pretended he couldn't care less. He stared out of the window at the passing hills and fields as the minibus bounced along, and he tried to ignore all the jumbled up feelings bouncing around him, deep down inside.

As the minibus came down the hill to Blue Flag Beach, Murphy stared

out across the sea. It was the very
first time he had ever seen the sea.
It was bigger and bluer and sparklier
than he had ever imagined.

It was a perfect beach day: warm
and breezy. The water glittered in
the early morning sunshine. The
car park was filling up. People and
dogs were spilling out of cars, with

surfboards, bags and towels, and buckets and spades. It was going to be busy on the beach today.

'NOW THEN, PUPS,' boomed Professor Offenbach, 'THIS IS A LIFEGUARDED BEACH, BUT TAKE NOTE OF THE DIFFERENT FLAGS. ONLY SWIM BETWEEN THE RED AND YELLOW STRIPED FLAGS, AND NO SWIMMING WHEN THE RED FLAG IS FLYING.'

'Come on,' yelled Star, climbing out of the minibus. 'Let's find a spot on the beach where we can watch the surf-dog championships later.'

Murphy stayed behind with Rodrigo and Major Bones while the other pups ran off across the beach with Professor Offenbach. Towards the far end of the beach, bright banners with WORLD JUNIOR SURF-DOG CHAMPIONSHIPS rippled in the breeze. Already there were lots of pups with surfboards of all shapes and sizes lined up on the sand.

The sea was calm. Small waves curled and ran along the shoreline.

'These waves are too tiny!' cried Rodrigo. 'I cannot surf on them!'

'Maybe the competition will be cancelled,' said Murphy. He secretly hoped it would be, so that Rodrigo wouldn't get the chance to show off in front of the other pups.

'Qué problema!' said Rodrigo. 'I have come so far for this.'

'Don't worry,' woofed Major Bones. The surf forecast says the wind will pick up. There will be some big waves this afternoon.'

'That is good news,' said Rodrigo. 'I've been looking forward to seeing Aliikai catch some waves.'

'Aliikai?' said Murphy. 'Who's Aliikai?'

'Aliikai?' said Rodrigo, flicking his mop of fur from his eyes. 'You haven't heard of her? She is the world junior surf-dog champion from Hawaii. She lives up to her name. It means Queen of the Sea.'

'Is she better than you?' said Murphy.

Rodrigo's eyes lit up. 'Amigo, she's the best. It would be an honour to surf on the same wave as her.'

'Right you two,' barked Major Bones at Murphy and Rodrigo. 'Come with me. It's the moment you've been waiting for. We're off to meet the world famous surf rescue dog, Boris of Bognor Regis.'

Murphy trotted across the sand, wagging his tail in excitement. He followed Major Bones up the wooden steps leading to the lifeguard hut.

The human lifeguards patted the

pups' heads as they passed.

'Pups!' announced Major Bones. 'May I introduce you to Boris of Bognor Regis.'

'Welcome to Blue Flag Beach,' said Boris.

Murphy just stared at his hero. He couldn't think of anything to say. The sea breeze lifted Boris's silky black fur and the sunlight glinted in his deep brown eyes.

The gold medal of gallantry around his neck shone out brightly. He looked even more magnificent than he did on TV.

Murphy closed his eyes and imagined Boris placing a gold medal around his own neck.

'Qué vista!' said Rodrigo.

'Yes,' agreed Boris. 'It's a fine view. From here we can see all along the beach. It's important to keep watch at all times.'

Murphy shook himself from his daydream and looked along the whole length of Blue Flag Beach. It stretched in a long curve of yellow sand between two headlands. The tide was in. The sea was calm and blue. It glittered and sparkled beneath the hot sun. Small waves curled and broke on the shore, foaming across the wet sand.

The beach was busy now. It was a patchwork of brightly coloured towels and stripy windbreaks. Murphy could see his puppy friends playing on the sand. Humans were everywhere too: sitting in deckchairs, playing ball games, flying kites. There were lots of people in the water, running in and out, jumping over the small waves, swimming, and lying on bodyboards. So many people, thought Murphy. How could Boris and the human lifeguards possibly watch over them all?

'So,' said Boris. 'Before we head out onto the water, let's have a little theory test.'

Murphy glanced at Rodrigo. He wanted to show Boris that he knew his stuff. He wanted to answer the questions before Rodrigo.

Boris pointed out to the sea with his huge paw. 'Tell me, young pups, what dangers are out there in the sea?'

Murphy shot his paw in the air. 'There might be weever fish beneath the sand?' he said.

'Very good,' said Boris. 'The spines of the weever fish fin can cause a very painful sting if stepped on. What else? What about the sea? Is it safe out there today?'

Murphy and Rodrigo looked up and down the beach. Murphy knew it was dangerous to swim around headlands because of strong currents, but the tide was right in. The sea was calm, and the waves were small. Rodrigo put his paw in the air, but Murphy answered before Rodrigo had a chance. 'It's quite safe out there,' said Murphy. 'It's perfect for swimming.'

'Young pup,' said Boris, clearing his throat. 'NEVER for one moment think the sea is safe. It may be a fun place to play, but there are ALWAYS dangers.'

'But . . . the sea looks so calm,' said Murphy.

Boris shook his head. 'Out there lies a DANGER. INVISIBLE. UNSEEN. Something with the power to take you out to sea.'

'Sharks?' said Murphy.

'I'm not talking about sharks,' said Boris. 'Let's see if Rodrigo has the right answer.'

Rodrigo put his paws on the wooden railings and pointed to the very far end of the beach. 'Over there,' he said, 'where the waves look a bit flattened. That might be a rip tide.'

'Well done,' beamed Boris. He held up a board with a diagram of a rip tide. 'And can you tell us what a rip tide is and what you do if you get stuck in one?'

Rodrigo cleared his throat. 'A rip tide is a fast-moving current of water that moves away from the beach. If you get caught in one, don't try to swim against it. You must swim along, level with the beach, until you are out of it, and then swim to shore.'

'Well done, well done,' said Boris patting Rodrigo on the back.

Murphy turned away and scowled. He wanted to prove he was better than Rodrigo. He had to find a way he could impress Boris too.

4

'So,' said Boris, 'what should a human do if they find themselves in trouble in the water?'

Murphy put his paw up. 'They should wave a hand in the air and shout for help.'

'Well done,' said Boris. 'Let's just spend a while looking out across the bay checking no one is in trouble.'

Murphy puffed out his chest in pride. He'd got an answer right. He stood at the top of the steps and surveyed the beach, just like his hero. He felt the sun on his back and breathed in the salt smell of the sea. This had to be the best job in the whole wide world. This was where he belonged. This was where he'd always wanted to be.

He watched humans eating their picnics. He looked beyond the puppies from the academy, who were lying on the sand, to a boy building a sandcastle on the beach. No one needed help today. Or did they?

Beyond the sandcastle, Murphy could see two small children yelling

and splashing in a big rock pool.
The water came right up to their
necks. One girl went under the
water and disappeared from sight.

She waved her hands wildly in the
air. The humans around her hadn't
even noticed. The children needed

help and they needed it now. Murphy glanced at Rodrigo and Boris, but they were looking the other way. Maybe this was his chance to prove himself. This was a real-life rescue.

Murphy leapt down the wooden steps and bounded across the beach. He felt the wind in his ears and the sand beneath his feet. This was it. This was his moment. This was when he would make Boris proud. His friends would see he was much better than Rodrigo. People would gather around him and cheer. He was Murphy, surf sea rescue pup: the hero of the day.

'Woof,' Murphy barked. 'I'm coming . . . Woof! Woof! Woof!'

The puppies from the academy scattered as sand flew up from Murphy's paws.

He slammed through the sandcastle.

He pounded through the picnics.

Nothing else mattered now, only the rescue.

Murphy took a flying leap and splashed into the middle of the rock pool. It wasn't deep at all. The water only came up to his knees. The girls screamed and scrambled out of the rock pool.

Murphy ran after them. 'Wait, wait,' he barked.

But the girls ran faster and faster. Murphy felt Boris grab his collar and pull him back. 'Not so fast, young pup. Don't scare them. They didn't need saving.'

Murphy stared after them. 'But the water looked so deep. It came up to their necks.'

'They were lying down,' Boris sighed.

Rodrigo and the other pups crowded around him. Murphy thought he heard a few of them sniggering.

'But the children were shouting and splashing and waving their arms in the air,' said Murphy. 'They needed help.'

Boris put a big paw on Murphy's shoulder. 'Children scream and shout on the beach. It's what they do. They are just having fun. You must learn to tell the difference between who is in trouble and who is just having a good time.'

'I told them to wait, but they just ran away even faster,' said Murphy.

Boris sighed. 'Humans can't understand our woofs and barks,' he said. 'You know that. The children were frightened of you charging at them like that.'

Murphy stared down at his own large paws. He'd messed up again.

He'd made a fool of himself in front
of Boris, and in front of his friends.
There was so much to learn. Maybe
he just wasn't good enough to
become a surf rescue dog. Maybe he
wasn't good at anything at all.

'Cheer up Murphy,' said Boris. 'It
was an easy mistake. Let's get in the
water and start your rescue training.
Would you like that?'

Murphy nodded. At least
swimming was one thing he knew
he could do.

'Good,' said Boris, 'but first, I will

need you to put on one of these.' He held up a water rescue jacket. 'This will help you float in rough seas, and these handles are for the human to hold on to. Hopefully both you and Rodrigo will earn your Surf Rescue badge today.

Boris checked that the human lifeguards were watching the beach and then he led Murphy and Rodrigo down to the water's edge.

'Right,' said Boris. 'I will swim out beyond the breaking waves and then wave my paws as the signal to rescue me. To earn your Surf Rescue badge, you must swim out to me and pull me back to shore. Is that clear?'

Murphy nodded. He'd trained
for this. He'd read all the books.
He was the best swimmer at the
academy. He'd rescued pups from
the swimming pool, and from the
river. He felt ready.

Almost.

The only thing he had never
done was swim in the sea!

Since they had arrived at the
beach, the wind had picked up and
the waves were bigger. White foam
crested at their tops.

The waves looked much bigger from the shoreline. They looked HUGE.

He didn't feel so sure about swimming in the sea now.

'Who wants to go first?' said Boris.

Murphy waited for Rodrigo to put his paw in the air.

'Good luck, Rodrigo,' said Boris.

As Boris trotted into the sea, a boy in a red baseball cap and Hawaiian shorts ran after him and tried to ride on his back.

'Save me! Save me!' the boy

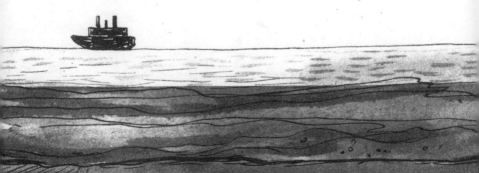

shouted.

Boris had to bark at him to make him let go. He left the boy in the shallows and swam out beyond the breaking waves. He faced the shore and put his paws in the air. This was the signal. He needed rescuing.

Rodrigo plunged into the water. He was only a little dog, but he paddled out though the waves. Wave after wave passed over Rodrigo. The little dog disappeared and bobbed up again, swimming out to Boris. Murphy watched as Boris

grabbed onto the handle on the water rescue jacket with his teeth and let Rodrigo pull him back to shore.

'Perfect!' woofed Boris when they were back on the beach. 'Textbook stuff. Well done.'

Rodrigo shook himself dry. 'Good luck,' he barked at Murphy.

Murphy looked out at the waves.

If Rodrigo could do it, surely he could? Rodrigo looked more like a lap dog than a water rescue dog.

The boy in the red baseball cap hadn't given up. He lay down in the shallow waves and kicked and thrashed in the water, pretending to be in trouble. 'Save me! Save me!' he yelled. Boris ignored him and swam back out into the sea.

Murphy waited until Boris gave the signal, and then he plunged in. He bounded over the waves in the shallows. But the water was getting deeper and the waves were getting higher. Soon Murphy was out of his depth. He kept losing sight of Boris behind each wave. Spray splashed in his eyes and the sea caught his legs and swirled him round. How had Rodrigo managed to keep on swimming in this?

One wave rose up in front of him. Up and up and up. Murphy tried to swim over the top of it, but it began to curl, and then folded on top of him, rolling him over and over and over. He closed his eyes. Water rushed into his mouth and up his nose. It was like being in a giant washing machine at full spin.

Round and round and round and

round and round he spun, until the
wave tumbled him all the way back
to the beach and dumped him on the
hard sand.

Murphy opened his eyes to see
Major Bones, Rodrigo, and all his
friends staring down at him.

'What happened?' said Star.

'Are you OK?' said Rodrigo.

Murphy groaned and closed his
eyes. He'd made a fool of himself
again. He couldn't get anything right.

Major Bones leaned down. 'Up
you get Murphy, and go back out into
the sea.'

Murphy looked out at the waves.

They looked even bigger than before. He didn't want to face the waves ever again. Not even the little ones. He didn't want to mess up again in front of his friends. He wasn't sure he even wanted to be a surf rescue dog any more. He had to face it. He was scared of the sea. 'I think I'll be a lifeguard at a swimming pool instead,' he said.

'Don't be silly,' said Star.

'Have another go,' said Scruff.

'No!' wailed Murphy.

Boris pushed his way through the pups. 'Do you want to try that again?'

Murphy covered his face with

his paws. He'd failed in front of his hero. What if he failed a second time? 'I'm not going back out there.'

'Amigo,' said Rodrigo, patting Murphy's back, 'do it for your friends.'

Murphy looked around them all and then glared at Rodrigo. 'They don't need me now, anyway, because they have you.'

'Murphy . . . !' said Star.

'Just leave me,' Murphy blurted out. He flung off his water rescue jacket, pushed his way through the pups, and ran and ran to the far end of the beach. He sank down behind the rocks, closed his eyes, and pressed his head against the sand, hoping it would swallow him up. His friends wouldn't think he was a hero any more. It was all over. All his dreams were crushed. He'd never be a surf rescue dog, not now, not ever.

Everything had gone horribly, horribly wrong.

5

Murphy lay quite still for a long time. He hoped everyone would forget about him and leave him there for ever.

Just as he was beginning to wonder if everyone *had* forgotten about him, a shadow passed across his face.

'Hey, amigo!'

Murphy opened one eye.

Rodrigo was standing over him,

leaning against his surfboard.

'What do you want, Rodrigo?'

'I came to see if you'd like to catch some heavies with me before the competition starts?'

'Heavies?' said Murphy.

'Sí! Let's go find ourselves some big waves.'

'I told you. I'm not going back in,' said Murphy. He stared at the waves thundering on the shore. 'I can't believe you actually like it out there.'

'I didn't always like it,' said Rodrigo.

'You didn't?' said Murphy.

'No,' said Rodrigo. He sat down next to Murphy on the sand. 'Where I come from, everyone surfs. When I first tried, the other dogs were always better than me. I wanted to be the best so much that I didn't enjoy just being out on the water. I kept falling off the big waves. I was frightened!'

'Then what happened?' said Murphy.

'Well, I stayed on the shore
while I watched my friends surfing.
Some were better than others, but
it didn't seem to bother them. They
were all having fun. I realised I
wasn't frightened of the waves. I was
frightened of failing. I was frightened
of not being the best.'

'So what did you do?'

'I figured that I didn't have to be
the best, but I had to try to be *my*
best,' said Rodrigo. 'Take Aliikai. I
may never be as good a surfer as she
is, but I can learn from her. Now I
just try to get a little bit better every
day, and, best of all, I have
fun with my friends too.'

70

Murphy stared at his paws for a long, long time. 'I'm sorry I haven't been very nice to you. I wanted to be the best too. And I wanted my friends to like me. I was worried they'd like you more.'

'Your friends *do* like you.'

Murphy turned around to Star's voice.

'Star!' said Murphy.

The other pups were there too.

'Of course we like you, Murphy,' said Pip.

'We don't like you just because you're great at water rescue,' said Star. 'You don't have to be a hero for us to want to be your friends. We like you because you're you.'

'But you've not been very nice since Rodrigo arrived,' said Scruff.

'I know,' said Murphy, 'and I'm sorry. Can you forgive me?' Murphy looked around at all his friends.

'Of course,' they barked.

'Thank you,' woofed Murphy. 'Thank you.'

'Hey, amigo!' said Rodrigo, slapping

Murphy on the back. 'Surf's up. C'mon. Hitch a ride with me.'

Murphy's paws trembled. The waves looked like big monsters rising up to eat him. 'I can't go back out there.'

'Go on,' said Star. 'You do want to be a surf rescue dog, don't you?'

Murphy swallowed hard and nodded. He wanted to be one more than anything in the world.

Rodrigo leaned in close. 'There is an old sea dog saying: *if you want to see what's on the other side of the ocean, you have to first leave the shore.*' Rodrigo held out a paw. 'It means that sometimes you have to be brave enough to take the first step.'

Murphy took Rodrigo's paw, and then followed him back along the beach and into the shallow waves.

'Hop up behind me,' said Rodrigo.

Murphy climbed behind Rodrigo on the surfboard. It wobbled, but he clung on, lying low, and they paddled out to sea.

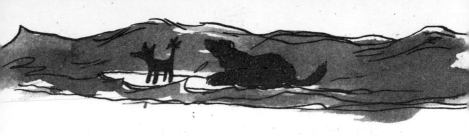

Rodrigo pointed to the breaking waves. 'Keep your head down when the breakers come at you and let them pass over,' he said. 'And if you meet a really big one, turn turtle!'

'Turn turtle?' said Murphy.

A huge wave curled over and its foam surged towards them.

'Sí,' said Rodrigo, 'like this. Hold on tight, amigo!' He flipped the board so they were underneath the surfboard as the wave passed over them. He flipped them back up again.

'That way you don't end up in a wipeout.'

Murphy watched the wave tumble on its way towards the shore.

Rodrigo paddled them out beyond the breaking waves and Murphy sat with him on the board, rising up and down in the swell.

Wave after wave rolled in from the ocean.

'You ready to catch a wave?' said Rodrigo.

'I've never tried surfing before,' said Murphy. 'Is it scary?'

'There's nothing like it,' said Rodrigo. 'You've got to listen to the ocean. Hear its voice inside of you. Become part of the wave; part of the ocean.'

Rodrigo paddled them towards the shore. He turned around to look at the oncoming waves. One big wave started to rise up and up behind them. 'This is our wave, amigo. Stay with me.'

Murphy paddled with Rodrigo. As the wave caught them the surfboard teetered on the crest, and then they were over the top of it, rushing down the other side, faster and faster. Murphy's ears streamed out behind him. The salty wind

ran through his fur. He felt like he
was flying. It was the best feeling in
the world. Nothing else mattered. He
knew what Rodrigo meant. He was
part of the wave; part of the ocean.

'ARRRRRROOO' howled Rodrigo.

'ARRRRRROOOO!' howled
Murphy.

They whizzed in a blur of dog and
surf towards the shore.

Murphy jumped off in the
shallows and bounced around the
surfboard. 'That was brilliant,' he
barked. 'Let's do it again.'

By the time Murphy and Rodrigo
heard Boris calling their names, they
had already ridden about twenty
waves.

'It seems you have mastered
the waves,' said Boris. 'Maybe you
should try for your Surf Rescue
badge after all. We just have time
for the test before the surf-dog
competition starts.'

Murphy couldn't believe his ears.
Maybe he could still be a surf rescue
dog. 'Thank you, Rodrigo,' he said.
'Thanks for everything.'

Major Bones and Rodrigo helped

Murphy into his water rescue jacket
again, while Boris swam out to be
rescued. The boy in the red baseball
cap was back, and tried even harder
to grab hold of Boris, but Boris just
shook him off and pushed him back
to the beach.

Murphy watched the boy wander
away down the shoreline with his
hands deep in the pockets of his

shorts, kicking the waves with his feet. He kept turning around, glaring moodily back at them.

Boris paddled out beyond the breaking waves. 'Right,' he barked. He bobbed up and down and waved his paws in the air. 'Come on, Murphy. Let's see what you can do.'

'HELP! HELP!'

Murphy turned to look further down the beach. The boy with the red baseball cap was in the water,

and he seemed to be quite far out.
The water was up to his neck and
the waves were crashing over him.
He disappeared for a moment then
came back up flailing his hands in
the air.

'HELP! HELP!'

Boris was already swimming
towards the boy. 'Stay on the
beach, pups,' he barked. 'This is an
emergency. This is the real thing.'

6

Murphy watched Boris paddle towards the boy. His thick black fur streamed out behind him. The boy went under again. Murphy held his breath. He was watching his hero in action. This was a real rescue. He hoped he would be as brave one day too.

People lined the shore and watched as Boris fought his way through the waves. He had almost reached the boy when the boy stood up. Boris soon found himself walking in shallow water too. They were on a sandbank, and the water was only ankle deep. The boy had only been pretending to be in trouble.

The boy started laughing and pointing at Boris, but Boris just turned and walked back to the shore. His fur dripped with water and seaweed, but he looked too cross to even shake himself off.

Back at the lifeguard hut, Boris shook himself dry. 'It's very dangerous to distract the emergency services like that. His silly game could have cost the lives of others.'

Murphy glanced back out to sea. The surf-dog competitors were lined up on the sand and a large golden retriever with sun-bleached fur looked ready to announce the start of the competition. 'What about my Surf Rescue badge?' asked Murphy.

Boris shook his head. 'I'm afraid we won't have time now, Murphy. The competition is about to begin and it will be too late afterwards to try.'

Murphy sighed. He had wanted to earn his Surf Rescue badge today. He followed Boris down the shore and helped him move the black and white chequered flags along the beach to show where the surfing competition would take place.

Murphy passed Rodrigo. 'I hope you win.'

'Thanks,' said Rodrigo. 'I hope so too, but look over there. That's Aliikai, the world champion.'

A small chihuahua was polishing a pink surfboard.

Murphy patted Rodrigo on the back. 'Good luck, amigo! Do your best.'

Murphy didn't sit with his friends.
He stayed on duty with Boris to
watch over the competition and
make sure none of the competitors
got into difficulties.

Murphy watched Rodrigo take his
turn. All the pups at the academy
cheered for him. Rodrigo paddled
out and caught a wave, slicing down
its breaking edge. He put in a couple
of good turns. It was good, but was it
good enough to win?

Dog after dog went up to surf.

Alfonso the affenpinscher from California wiped out under a big wave.

Lara the lurcher from Cornwall tipped the front of her board into a wave and went flying through the air.

All the time the waves were getting bigger and bigger.

'Look,' said Boris. 'It's Aliikai's turn now.'

Everyone on the beach clapped and cheered as Aliikai made her way down to the water's edge. Excitement rippled across the

crowd. They were about to see the
world champion in action. No one
wanted to miss this. All eyes were
on the small chihuahua and the
pink surfboard as Aliikai paddled
out into the waves.

Murphy surveyed the beach.
No one else was in the water.
Everyone had gathered to watch the
competition. The sea was empty.

Empty, except for one boy . . . the boy in the red baseball cap.

The boy was in the water at the far end of the beach, waving his arms in the air.

'Look,' said Murphy. 'That boy's calling for help again.'

Boris stared across the beach.

'Hmmph!' he said. 'The cheek of it. He's mucking about again wanting attention. Best ignore him. He'll come out when he's bored.'

Boris trotted away to make sure he was in a position to help Aliikai if she needed it.

But Murphy couldn't ignore the
boy. He was waving his hands wildly
above his head. Murphy was sure he
was calling out too, although the
wind was blowing away from him,
carrying the boy's voice further down
the beach in the other direction.

A colder wind was blowing,
ruffling Murphy's fur.

The boy kept on yelling. His head
bobbed under the water and up
again. The waves were getting bigger
and the tide had gone further out.
Murphy felt a knot of worry tighten
in his stomach. He glanced back at

the surf competition. Maybe he should stop the competition and call Boris and the lifeguards. But Boris had said the boy was trying to fool them again. Surely Boris was right.

Murphy felt uneasy. He felt it deep down in his chest. His paws twitched. Maybe he would just take a walk along the beach and check the boy was OK. He could be back before Aliikai had finished her turn.

Murphy turned and trotted down the far end of the beach. The waves were different here. They didn't curl in a soft line but reared up in messy waves that thumped down on the sand. As Murphy watched, the boy seemed to be drifting further and further out, as if invisible hands were pulling him away from the shore.

Murphy knew the boy wasn't fooling around any more. This boy was in deep, deep trouble.

This boy was in a rip tide and being sucked out to sea.

Murphy didn't even think about it. He plunged into the water.

The first wave hit him, rolling him over, but he got up again and bounded further into the water. He

remembered Rodrigo telling him to keep his head down and let the waves pass over him. He plunged through the water, diving underneath each mountain of wave. He could feel the rip current take hold of him and pull him too. He glanced back and watched the beach disappear further and further away.

Keep calm, he told himself. Don't panic. He had to find the boy. The boy was underwater again. Murphy

couldn't see him, but he felt him
with his paws. The boy held onto
Murphy and pulled himself up again.

He took a huge gasp as his head
burst above the water.

'Woof,' Murphy barked. The
boy's hand reached up and grasped
the handles on Murphy's jacket, and
together they spun in the rip tide,
heading out to sea.

Murphy knew it was hopeless
to swim against the rip tide. He
had to swim out of it, level with
the shoreline.

He could see people running along the beach towards them; Boris out in front, and all his friends not far behind.

Murphy turned and swam level with the beach. His legs ached. Water rushed up his nose and into his eyes, but he kept swimming until he felt the pull of the rip tide weaken. Now all he had to do was to swim to the shore. It was harder with the weight of the boy, and the waves seemed even bigger.

Murphy looked behind him to see a huge wave rise up. Everything slowed down. He thought of Rodrigo and how he had told him not to fight the ocean

but to become part of it. He didn't
feel frightened any more.

'Hold on,' Murphy woofed. He
pushed his paws in front of him as
the wave curled over, and raced
them, bodysurfing, to the shore.

'ARRRRRRROOOOOO!'
howled Murphy.

People were cheering along the shoreline. Boris bounded in and helped Murphy and the boy onto the sand.

'Well done, young pup,' woofed Boris. 'Well done.'

The boy's mother rushed up and held her son in her arms.

Murphy's friends crowded around him. He was wet and cold, and plastered in sand and seaweed.

'You're safe, Murphy,' cried Scruff.

'We thought we'd lost you,' said Pip.

'You're our hero,' said Rodrigo.

Murphy smiled.

He smiled because he knew it didn't matter if he was a hero or not, his friends were there for him, and that meant more than anything in the world.

7

There was a buzz of excitement at
the puppy academy.

All the puppies filled the hall
and waited. It wasn't every day
that a world famous celebrity visited
the academy. Murphy sat next to
Rodrigo and his friends and waited
for Boris of Bognor Regis.

'Here he comes,' woofed Star.

All the pups howled with excitement
as Boris walked into the hall.

'WELCOME, WELCOME EVERYONE TO THE FRIDAY AWARD CEREMONY,' barked Professor Offenbach, 'TODAY WE WELCOME BORIS OF BOGNOR REGIS TO PRESENT SOME VERY SPECIAL BADGES. WE ALSO SAY A VERY SAD FAREWELL TO OUR MEXICAN STUDENT, RODRIGO LOPEZ. I KNOW MANY OF YOU HAVE BECOME GREAT FRIENDS WITH HIM AND WILL KEEP IN CONTACT. WHO KNOWS, MAYBE SOME OF YOU WILL EVEN GET THE CHANCE TO VISIT HIM IN MEXICO ONE DAY.'

Murphy looked at Rodrigo. 'I don't want you to go,' he said.

Rodrigo wagged his tail. 'Amigo, come and visit me any time. The surf is great in Mexico!'

'AND . . . ' continued Professor Offenbach, **'I WOULD LIKE TO**

CALL UP RODRIGO TO THE
GIANT SAUSAGE PODIUM
AND GIVE HIM A BAG OF
SURFBOARD-SHAPED CRUNCHIE
MUNCHIES IN CELEBRATION
OF HIS FIFTH PLACE AT THE
WORLD JUNIOR SURF-DOG
CHAMPIONSHIPS.'

All the pups cheered and
thumped their tails on the floor for
Rodrigo, but none thumped their
tail more loudly than Murphy.

'I WOULD NOW LIKE TO ASK
BORIS TO PRESENT RODRIGO
WITH THE SURF RESCUE
BADGE.'

Murphy watched Boris fix the
badge to Rodrigo's collar. He sighed.
He wished he'd been able to take the
test too.

'**AND I WOULD LIKE TO CALL
UP MURPHY TO THE SAUSAGE
PODIUM TOO, TO RECEIVE AN
AWARD.**'

Murphy didn't move.

'Go on,' prodded Star.

'But I didn't take the test,' said
Murphy.

Boris faced all the puppies. 'Murphy made a few mistakes during his training. We all make mistakes. The important thing is to learn from them. I made the mistake of thinking a boy was fooling around again in the water. It was Murphy who trusted his instincts and did something incredibly brave. He risked his own life to save someone else's.'

Silence fell across the hall.

Boris cleared his throat. 'Because of his bravery in the face of extreme danger, I would like to present Murphy with the highest honour . . .'

Murphy looked up to see Boris
holding a gold medal in his paw . . .
'The gold medal for gallantry.'

All the puppies thumped their
tails and howled.

Murphy's legs were shaking,
but he made his way up onto
the podium. He looked into the
Newfoundland's brave eyes. 'You're
my hero,' Murphy
whispered.

Boris of Bognor Regis placed the medal around Murphy's neck and smiled. 'You're *my* hero too.'

'One last swim in the river,' woofed Rodrigo, jumping into the water with Pip and Scruff.

Murphy sat with Star on the riverbank.

'I'm going to miss him,' said Murphy.

'Me too,' said Star.

Major Bones sat down beside them. 'Well done on your medal for gallantry,' he said. 'You were very brave indeed.'

Murphy stared at his feet. 'Anyone would have done the same,' he said.

'Maybe,' said Major Bones. 'It was brave to swim out into those waves and save that boy. But courage comes in different forms. It was brave to get back up and go out into the waves when you were scared to try again. Not many would have given it another go.'

'Rodrigo helped me with that,'

said Murphy. He sighed. 'I feel so bad about being unfriendly to him when he arrived.'

Star looked up at him. 'You said you were sorry.'

'Yes,' smiled Major Bones. 'And it can take even greater courage, to say sorry and to admit that you were wrong.'

Rodrigo splashed water at Murphy and Star. 'Hey! Amigos! Aren't you coming in?'

'We're coming,' yelled Star.

'WATCH OUT,' woofed Murphy.

A huge brown blur whizzed through the air . . .

'ARRROOOOOOOOOOOO. . . '

MORE PUPPY ACADEMY stories!

GILL LEWIS
PUPPY ACADEMY

ILLUSTRATED BY
SARAH HORNE

Scout
AND THE SAUSAGE THIEF

GILL LEWIS
PUPPY ACADEMY

STAR
ON STORMY MOUNTAIN

GILL LEWIS
PUPPY ACADEMY

PIP
AND THE PAW OF FRIENDSHIP

Meet WHIZZ, A REAL LIFE WATER RESCUE DOG!

NAME
Whizz

OCCUPATION
Water rescue and therapy dog

LIKES
Company and cuddles

HATES
Hot weather, because he has a really thick double coat

Whizz is really lively and excited when leaping to the rescue but as soon as he spends time with a sick child he changes into a lovely calm cuddly friend.

MISSION STATEMENT

Newfound Friends is a charity that works with Newfoundland dogs. The dogs help children to learn about water safety as well as raising money for children's charities. Out of the water they are wonderful therapy dogs for children who are disabled or very unwell.

Newfound Friends UK
Registration number 1163201
Find out more at www.newfoundfriends.co.uk

WATER RESCUE DOG FACTS!

DID YOU KNOW?

Leonbergers like Murphy and Newfoundlands like Boris make great water rescue dogs, because of their size, stamina, and their love of water!

 Water rescue dogs sometimes have to tow boats.

DID YOU KNOW?

They also have to practise jumping off different types of boat.

The handle on a water rescue jacket has two uses: for the person being rescued to hold on to, and to help lift the dog back into a lifeboat.

DID YOU KNOW?

Leonbergers and Mexican hairless dogs have flaps of skin between their toes, giving them webbed feet like a duck! This means they are excellent swimmers.

DID YOU KNOW?

Another name for a Mexican hairless dog like Rodrigo is a xoloitzcuintli (say "show-low-eats-queent-lee")

Leonbergers have oily fur and two layers of coat, which helps to keep them warm in the water.

I'm **MURPHY**, a Leonberger, just like Murphy in this book. He's named after me. I LOVE people and I LOVE water, which is why Leonbergers make such great water rescue dogs. Sometimes when I meet people I get so excited, I forget just how big I am. But I'm a big dog with a big heart, which is why people seem to find me very huggable.

If you want me, I'll be there with you. I'll come on all your adventures. I'll climb mountains and swim across rivers with you. I'm so strong, I'll even carry your picnic too.

Here are some other stories we think you'll love...

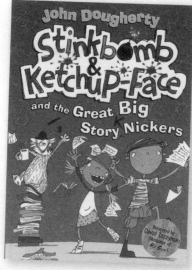

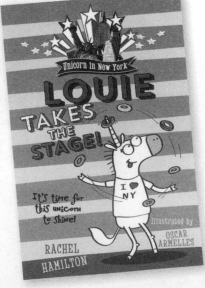